Whispers in the Dark:

A Techno-Haunting Novella

R.G. Clark

Published by PleaseLetThemKnow, L.L.C.
Dover, Delaware

For permissions, inquiries, or information, please contact: PleaseLetThemKnow, L.L.C.
Email: info@pleaseletthemknow.com

ISBN: 978-1-964580-37-1 (Paperback)
ISBN: 978-1-964580-45-6 (E-book)
ISBN: 978-1-964580-46-3 (Hardcover)

Printed in the United States of America
First Edition: 2025

Dedication

I want to dedicate this book to all the passionate fans of the horror genre. Since my grade school days, I have found immense joy in reading the captivating novels of Stephen King. His remarkable storytelling has deeply inspired me, and while I may not be in the same league as the greats, I hope to share our love for tales that evoke both fear and fascination!

Acknowledgments

I want to express my sincere gratitude to my mother, sister, and friends, whose unwavering support inspires me every day. I also thank the brilliant horror authors like Stephen King, who ignited my creative passion. Furthermore, shows like The Outer Limits, The Twilight Zone, A Haunting, and Fringe have gifted me with thrilling experiences, fueling my drive to pursue my dreams in writing and storytelling.

Table of Contents

Whispers in the Dark:
A Techno-Haunting Novella
R.G. Clark

Overview
Whispers in the Dark: A Techno-Haunting Novella

Prepare to be captivated by a thrilling journey through the unsettling yet captivating world of techno-horror in this electrifying collection of five interconnected stories set in Trenton, New Jersey. Each tale dives headfirst into the spine-tingling clash between cutting-edge digital technology, Artificial Intelligence, and the chilling presence of the supernatural, creating a web of interconnected narratives that will keep you on the edge of your seat.

From sleep-tracking apps that unveil more than just your rest patterns to AI devices that seem all too aware, this novella weaves a mesmerizing tapestry of urban anxiety.

Filled with the vibrant energy of 70s music and deep, moody jazz undertones, these stories provide the perfect blend of eerie fun to keep you glancing over your shoulder. Prepare for a thrilling journey that will leave you breathless and questioning the very fabric of reality!

Meet the unforgettable characters:

Story 1: REM Sleep

Kelli, a night shift nurse in Trenton, NJ, experiences disturbing dreams after she starts using a sleep-tracking app. During her investigation into a fellow nurse's past, she uncovers a frightening connection between their technology and the spirit world.

Story 2: Spectral Scanner

Jared, a paranormal enthusiast, ventures into the abandoned Trenton Psychiatric Hospital armed with a ghost-hunting app. As he delves deeper into the hospital's troubling history and his mother's previous associations with it, he finds the boundary between reality and the supernatural becoming increasingly blurred.

Story 3: The Silence Between the Notifications

Riya, a dedicated marketing executive based in Lawrenceville, NJ, encounters unusual smartphone notifications following a high-pressure boardroom presentation. These cryptic alerts trigger memories of her late sister and suggest a spiritual message that Riya has been reluctant to confront. As she navigates this unexpected situation, her modern, technology-driven life transforms into a complex and haunting journey.

Story 4: REM Loop

Gary, who lives on Hoffman Avenue in Trenton, uses a sleep app to help him sleep better, but it starts recording ghostly whispers and puzzling messages. As his dreams turn increasingly aggressive and digital files suggest a concealed family secret, he realizes that something may be using his device to breach reality.

Story 5: The Box

Upon receiving an enigmatic AI media box, the narrator experiences frightening late-night disturbances. The device predicts violent events before they occur and seems to possess intimate knowledge about his neighbors and personal life.

The distinction between being an observer and a target blurs when the screen reflects aspects of his home life.

These characters are bound together by more than mere coincidence. The concept of digital residue links them—the notion that emotions, guilt, trauma, and even souls can linger on the devices we use every day. This novella challenges readers to confront the chilling possibilities that emerge when technology meets the supernatural.

Introduction

There was a time when the unknown thrived in forests, old houses, and condemned hospitals. Now, it resides in our pockets. We no longer gaze into mirrors to summon evils; instead, we gaze into screens—glowing rectangles that track our sleep, hear our voices, follow our movements, and whisper back to us in silence. This book ventures beyond traditional ghosts. It explores the traces we leave behind—in code, memory, and primarily, guilt. It reveals apps that open more than just programs, devices that capture more than just data, and questions we never intended to pose... until they are answered.

In Whispers in the Dark, you will meet five individuals—each unique and quite unaware that they are being drawn into something much older than their devices.

Their interactions with new technologies blur the line between the digital and the supernatural. Not every haunting begins with a knock at the door; some commence with a notification.

So, read on with an open mind. Be aware that some code may remain active even after the book or screen has closed. Some echoes reach back. And sometimes, when you listen intently... it listens back.

Story 1:
REM Sleep

Setting: Trenton, New Jersey
Main Character: Kelli, a nurse at St. Francis Medical Center

Kelli adjusted the collar of her scrubs and stepped out into the damp night air of Trenton. The streetlights flickered, and in the distance, a saxophone wept a haunting tune from a second-story window — moody, modern jazz interwoven with faint echoes of '70s soul. That was Trenton — a city stitched with rhythm and grit.

She had just finished another double shift at St. Francis, her third this week. The floors were short-staffed, and Kelli was grinding hard — saving up for her next certification. Her dream was to specialize in sleep studies or behavioral health. But lately, the irony wasn't lost on her: she couldn't sleep to save her life.

She became obsessed. She dug into DeepDream's origins and discovered it had been developed using EEG (Electroencephalogram) data from a now-defunct sleep lab in Ewing — just outside Trenton. The building had burned down in a freak fire over a decade ago. Only one name was loosely associated with the final patient intake list: Kayla Rivera.

Kelli found a digital archive article about the fire. Among the listed was a picture of a little girl, eyes wide and unreadable. That face — unmistakable. It was the girl from her dreams.

Driven, she looked into public records. Kayla's parents still lived in the area — in Lawrence Township. Kelli, heart pounding, reached out by email under the guise of conducting health research related to sleep patterns.

To her surprise, Mrs. Rivera replied.

They had been experiencing strange phenomena: old toys moving on their own, the scent of lavender — Kayla's favorite — lingering in her untouched bedroom. And worse, both parents reported hearing her voice through their phones late at night. "It's like she's trapped in something," Mrs. Rivera wrote.

Kelli arranged a visit.

The Riveras' home was a modest ranch house tucked away on a quiet street lined with sycamores. The moment Kelli stepped inside, she felt it — a static tension in the air, like the pause between notes in an unresolved jazz riff.

The house smelled faintly of vanilla and something older — charred wood, maybe. In Kayla's room, nothing had been moved. Dolls sat on the shelf, untouched. A music box on the dresser opened on its own and played a warped version of "Twinkle, Twinkle, Little Star."

Mrs. Rivera looked haunted. Mr. Rivera barely spoke.

"She always had vivid dreams," Mrs. Rivera whispered, clutching a faded photo of Kayla in a red dress. "Now I hear her voice... asking for someone. A nurse, I think. She keeps saying, 'She listens. She listens.'"

Back in her apartment, Kelli tried to shut it all out. But her dreams now bled into waking hours. She'd see Kayla's reflection in windows or hear her name whispered over the hospital intercom when no call had been made.

Her eyes became sunken. Her walk was unsteady. Coworkers noticed, but no one said anything.

One morning, she awoke standing in her kitchen, unsure of how she had gotten there. Her sleep tracker showed a whole night of rest — and yet, she felt like she hadn't slept at all.

Then came the third dream — the final descent. Kelli found herself inside St. Francis Hospital, but it was submerged beneath the water. Light flickered from above the surface as though the ceiling were an ocean. Paper charts floated past her. Her scrubs clung to her like a second skin. She tried to breathe, but there was no panic — just pressure and music.

From somewhere deep in the halls, a broken melody played. It was What's Going On, but slowed down until it became unrecognizable, mournful, like a lullaby sung by a ghost.
She turned a corner and saw a figure seated in a wheelchair.

It was Kayla.

Except now she was older — maybe thirteen. Her eyes were sunken, her skin pale and translucent, glowing slightly like a phosphorescent deep-sea creature. She turned toward Kelli with a slow, jerky motion, like a puppet on a string.

"I didn't want to burn," she whispered. Kelli backed away, but the hallway stretched and tilted, gravity breaking apart. She stumbled toward the elevator, pressing the call button frantically.

The doors opened. Inside was her own hospital bed — the one from her apartment, soaked in seawater, covered in vines.

She stepped in.

When the doors closed, everything went black. She woke up gasping, tangled in damp sheets, salt on her lips. Then came the night the speaker turned on by itself.

A slowed version of Me and Mrs. Jones groaned through distorted speakers. Her phone vibrated with a new notification from DeepDream:

"Kayla has joined your sleep session." She screamed.

In the final recording, Kelli appears still —
lying in bed, eyes open. The screen glitches. Her
voice, now low and warbled, whispers:

"I found her. I'm bringing her back."

The saxophone fades into static.

Outside, a single streetlamp buzzes and dies.

Addendum: Nurse's Note (Unfiled)

Source: Unfiled voice memo transcribed from a private sleep journal, recovered from the discarded locker of Kelli [Last Name Redacted], St. Francis Hospital, Trenton, NJ
Date: Unknown
File: 0035-REM-Continued.wav (Auto-tagged, not manually saved)

"I experienced another unsettling night. It's different now—this is no longer merely dreaming. It feels as if I'm... transported to another realm. I can hear Kayla's soft breaths beside me. I wake up drenched in sweat, yet the sheets are icy cold. Her chart has vanished from the system, but at times, I can still hear her patient ID echoed over the intercom.

The mattress logs suggest I've been awake the entire night. Yet, I distinctly remember sleeping.

I revisited the audio file—a recording I claimed I deleted. Beneath my voice, a chilling whisper emerges: 'You're next.'

I can't shake the feeling that I'm still trapped in a dream. I just... never truly awoke. The sense of isolation is palpable.

(End of memo. No further entries were recovered.)

Story 2: Spectral Scanner

Setting: Trenton & Ewing, New Jersey
Main Character: Jared, a freelance sound engineer and paranormal hobbyist

Jared had always been fascinated with the paranormal — not in a campy, Halloween way, but with a deep curiosity sparked from childhood. He grew up hearing whispered stories about the old State Lunatic Asylum at Trenton, later known as Trenton Psychiatric Hospital. His own mother had worked there as a nurse in the late '70s and early '80s. She never said much, but when she did, it was always accompanied by a somber pause... and the phrase:

"Some of those screams weren't from patients. They were from the walls."

Now in his mid-thirties and living in nearby Ewing, Jared had turned that curiosity into action. He freelanced as a sound engineer for podcasts and indie film crews, which provided him with access to high-end audio equipment. But on weekends, he turned his tools toward ghost-hunting.

He attended paranormal events up and down the East Coast — most recently the ParaUnity Expo in Woodbridge, where he met legends like the Ghost Brothers and members of the original Ghost Hunters team. His small YouTube channel, Phantom Feedback, had built a cult following. EVP (Electronic Voice Phenomena) was his specialty.

One day, a sponsor sent him a prototype ghost-hunting app: Spectral Scanner. It paired with any microphone and claimed to isolate paranormal frequencies using AI-assisted filtering.

He rolled his eyes. But still, he tested it.

The first scan was uneventful. He tried it in his apartment — nothing but static. Then he drove out to the overgrown backlot of the Trenton Psychiatric Hospital. The abandoned wings had long since been fenced off, but Jared knew the cracks in the chain link and the ways to sneak around the patrols.

That night, under a moonless sky, he placed his mic on a concrete bench and booted up the app.

The screen pulsed with soft blue rings. For minutes, nothing happened. Then — static cut through, followed by a whispery voice: "I'm still cold..."

Jared froze. The app transcribed the message in real time. "I'm still cold."

Goosebumps erupted on his neck. He rewound the recording — it was clear. Female. Tired. And definitely not from a living throat.

He returned the next night.

On his third visit, the app displayed a new message before he even hit RECORD:

"Welcome back, Jared."

He hadn't input his name. At first, he thought it was a marketing trick.

However, when he checked the app's permissions, he found no access to contacts or GPS. There was no reason it should know who he was — or where.

As the wind rustled the brittle grass around the lot, he pressed RECORD again.

"Help me."

"The door burned shut."

"He's here now..."

Each whisper grew more desperate. They always came from the same direction — the south wing, sealed since the fire in 1984. Jared's mother had worked that shift, though she never spoke of the incident.

He finally asked her about it. They sat in her kitchen, surrounded by vintage doilies and fading wallpaper. She hesitated, then poured them both tea. Her hands trembled.

"I heard a voice that night. Not screaming. Singing. A child, humming some lullaby. But when I followed it, the hallway was on fire. And yet, I still heard it — from inside the flames." She looked at him then, her eyes glassy.

"Don't go back there."

Of course, Jared did.

On his fifth visit, Spectral Scanner glitched —
the UI changed colors, now pulsing deep red.
The signal strength surged as he approached the
south wing's broken side door. His camera
caught a heat signature — faint but moving.

Then his audio feed erupted with layered
voices — screams, gasps, prayers — all
overlapping. Through it all, one voice cut
through:

"Let him see."

The door, once rusted shut, creaked open
two inches. Inside was pitch black. His
flashlight flickered. The app interface collapsed
into code — scrolling lines of text, symbols, and
what appeared to be old patient ID numbers.
Then, a final phrase appeared:

"He belongs now."

He turned to run, but the door slammed
shut. The sound in his headphones spiked — not
just voices now, but something else.

Breathing.

Behind him.

When he turned, the thermal lens showed a shape — tall, humanoid, but shuddering like static. Its "head" seemed fractured, split by dark bands. No eyes. Just a mouth opening wide.

He blacked out.

He awoke at home, bruised and disoriented.

The gear was in his apartment, but the recordings were corrupted, all except one image — a screenshot from the app, now unusable.

In it: his face. But altered. His eyes were blackened, and from his mouth leaked the same red waveform from the app interface.

His YouTube account was deleted days later — not by him.

He still hears static when he sleeps.

And sometimes, his door is open in the morning.

Epilogue:
Blog Post –
"Digital Residue"

Thread Title: Trenton Scanner Logs — EVP Nightmare?
Posted by: ghost recon | Forum: TechHaunt Logs

I reverse-engineered an old Android APK that someone anonymously posted on a sound engineering forum. Claimed it was an early test build of something called Spectral Scanner. When I ran it in a sandbox, it auto-linked to a buried GPS node near Trenton State Hospital. Audio logs included whisper fragments: "Let him see," "Still here," and a digital voice repeating:

"More to come..."

The metadata was tagged with one name: JARED. The scary part?
Every time I delete the file — it returns.

Story 3:
The Silence Between Notifications

Setting: Lawrenceville, New Jersey
Main Character: Riya, a marketing executive

Riya never had trouble tuning out the world —
not with her schedule. As one of the top
regional marketing leads for a fast-rising tech
firm, she built her success on control: daily
agendas, color-coded apps, and unread
notifications always count at zero.
So when the first strange notification appeared,
she assumed it was spam.

Don't look behind you.

It was 2:11 a.m. She had just put down her Kindle and turned off the lamp. Her phone lit up with the message despite being set to Do Not Disturb.

She scoffed, took a screenshot, and sent it to IT the next morning. But they found no record of any push activity. "Probably adware," they said. "Maybe something from an old app."

But then came another.

You're not alone.

It buzzed while she was mid-presentation. She ignored it and finished her pitch — though her delivery had noticeably shifted. Her tone became clipped and distracted, and when she ended with an abrupt "Any questions?" a few coworkers exchanged curious glances.

Something about her felt... off.

Then she opened her phone in the break room.

No trace. No app history. Just a rising sense of unease. Later, she noticed something else. In every moment of silence — the pause between meetings, the lull before a Zoom loaded — there was a faint sound. Like static. Or whispering.

The worst came during a late meeting on her laptop. Her coworker froze on the screen mid-sentence. Then, without warning, the video glitched, and for two full seconds, her face appeared in his Zoom window — but with hollow eyes and a twisted smile.

She slammed her laptop shut.

It wasn't until she dug through her phone settings that she discovered something even more disturbing: the device had previously been registered under another name. The original owner? A man named Ian Reid — a known EVP researcher who died five years ago under mysterious circumstances while working with ghost-hunting equipment in abandoned buildings across New Jersey.

And now, Riya was hearing whispers through the silence.

She wasn't just haunted.

She was connected.

That night, the notifications returned.

Stay awake. Don't trust the quiet.

She left her phone on the kitchen counter and walked away, trying to ignore it. But the microwave glitched, cycling rapidly through numbers before cutting off. Her Spotify playlist froze mid-song. Then, I played a reversed version of the track — whispery and layered with static.

She picked up the phone. The screen lit up without touch.

We see you now.

The whispering grew louder. Her smart speaker responded to no commands but occasionally muttered her name in a warped female voice. The lights dimmed. She caught herself standing in the hallway mirror, staring — except her reflection wasn't staring back. It smiled.

The haunting triggered a memory — one that Riya had buried under years of therapy and professional advancement.

Her sister, Sheila, had died when they were teenagers. A car crash. Sudden. Violent. But what haunted Riya more than the accident was what came before it—the silence, a fight over something petty. The last words they shared were sharp, unforgiving.

Sheila had always been more spiritual. She believed in signs, in energy, in speaking to the dead. Riya, the logical one, had dismissed it all as nonsense. But now the whispers in her apartment sounded eerily like Sheila's voice — soft, musical, insistent.

Once, years ago, Sheila had joked:

"If I ever die, I'm haunting you. Not to scare you — to get your attention. You never listen." Riya was listening now.

One evening, as Riya passed her hallway, every framed photo on the wall tilted simultaneously — as if nudged by an invisible hand. Her phone buzzed once.

Remember her.

Later that night, she found her smart TV playing footage of her home that she didn't recognize. Two girls — one unmistakably her, younger, full of energy. The other was Sheila. Laughing. Dancing. The footage jittered, skipping ahead to a moment where young Riya stormed out of frame, and Sheila sat quietly alone, staring directly into the camera. Mouth moving.

Whispering.

Riya muted the TV.

The whispers didn't stop.

She unplugged the device.

It kept playing.

Her hands shook. She turned to grab her phone — and the message was already there: "You're almost ready."

That night, Riya had had enough. She packed her phone into a shoebox, taped it shut, and drove to Mercer Meadows just outside of town. The trees loomed tall and watchful as she pulled off the gravel path and walked into the clearing with a hammer in hand. She didn't wait. She crushed the box with the first strike — cardboard collapsing, glass cracking, the phone's shell splitting apart.

She struck again.

And again.

The screen bled blue and black. The camera lens popped off and landed beside a pinecone. But just as she dropped the hammer and stepped back, her smartwatch — still synced — buzzed against her wrist.

"Thank you."

She froze.

The screen of the broken phone flickered one final time, barely holding on. Her face reflected in the cracked surface — but the eyes weren't hers.

They were Sheila's.

The reflection smiled.

Riya didn't scream. She didn't run. She sank to her knees, unable to look away. The phone finally went dark.

Epilogue:
"Digital Residue"

Thread Title: EVP Patterns in App-Corrupted Devices?
Posted by: modded harmonics | Forum: AudioGhostTech | Date: [Archived]

So I picked up a used smart speaker from a friend in Lawrenceville — brand-new condition, barely used. But here's the weird part: after setting it up, I started hearing faint audio under the regular output. Not voices exactly, but hums... layered like multiple people trying to speak at once.

I checked the logs. Hidden file paths. One audio file labeled "Sheila." Another? "Listen_9PM."

I traced the source to a sync history with a device registered to a former tech exec — name withheld for privacy — who supposedly disappeared after a mental break.

The last known transmission from her smartwatch read:

"Thank you."

Has anyone else had interference from a synced device after destroying the source? Thread flagged for review. Temporarily closed.

Story 4:
REM Loop

Setting: Hoffman Avenue, Trenton, New Jersey
Main Character: Gary (a thinly veiled
pseudonymous version of the author)

Gary had always been a light sleeper, but lately, sleep had started to feel like a trap. It began innocently enough—with a popular sleep-monitoring app that tracked breathing, snoring, and rest cycles. It was a tool for wellness, a techy lullaby, and fun to monitor.

But something else was listening, too.

His rowhouse on Hoffman Avenue was modest but held his family's weight. His late father's ashes sat on the mantle in a dark cherry urn, always in peripheral view. His father had loved authentic jazz — the kind that wrapped itself around your bones. Gary played it most nights, letting vinyl echoes of Stanley Turrentine or David Sanborn soften the walls while the app recorded the sounds of slumber.

At first, he checked the audio out of curiosity. Breathing. Snoring. A cough.

But one night, he heard… something else.

"Gary. Are you listening?"

He stared at the waveform. There was no cough, no rustle. Just a low voice, clear and slow, buried under a snore spike. It didn't sound like him. It didn't sound like anyone alive. He tried to dismiss it. Until the next night.

"You see it too, don't you?"

Gary hadn't slept deeply since, and each night brought new phrases. One time, the recording started before he hit the bed. Another time, it ended with the creak of his bedroom door — even though it had stayed shut all night.

But it wasn't just the recordings. It was what he saw out of the corner of his eye. A shadow horned and crouching — a ghostly devil shape. Sometimes on the floor. Sometimes perched on the edge of his dresser. But every time Gary turned to face it fully, it vanished like a playful (but menacing child). But this looked like no child.

Was it malicious? Curious? A figment of exhausted imagination? Or was it just a nightmare? He heard from a friend that some medications cause very crazy and violent dreams. He didn't believe that either. The recordings didn't help. They got weirder.

"It's not just your dream."

"He's still here. Right there. In the ashes."

One file played in reverse automatically. When Gary ran it through an editing app, it sounded like a scream embedded inside a whisper. He stopped listening in bed and started doing it in the morning. But even that didn't help. The night would still find him. He started researching. Paranormal boards. EVP forums. He posted anonymously. One user responded:

"Some apps don't just record sleep. They record presence. Yours is hearing something because you're living in it. If your dad's ashes are still there... you might not be alone."

He laughed it off.

Until the dream.

It was jazz again — "Pearls" by David Sanborn — but warped, slowed like it was playing through the water. In the dream, he was in his room, standing over himself. A shadow leaned over the bed, its face near his sleeping head. The urn pulsed with dull red light. Then the shadow turned — and it had his father's eyes.

He woke up soaked in sweat. The app had recorded seven minutes of static. Then, just at the end, one word:

"Home."

Gary stopped using the sleep app for three nights. He unplugged his phone and left it on the kitchen table like a cursed object. But even then, the dreams came. And without the recordings to contain them, they expanded. He was in his room again. Only now was it inverted — ceiling below, floor above, furniture nailed to the air like surrealist art. The devil-thing crawled sideways along the walls, moving like a glitch, limbs jerking with every breath of jazz from his speakers. Oddly, I wondered if it liked jazz.

It had no skin, not really. Its flesh was translucent, like wet plastic over raw muscle. Its head elongated, tapering toward curling, barbed horns that dripped like candle wax. Its eyes — if they were eyes — flickered like loading symbols, constantly rotating, never blinking. Worse than the sight was the sound it made. A gurgling chuckle layered over saxophone notes, like something trying to mimic laughter through a drainpipe. Gary tried to scream when it crawled toward him, but no sound came. He reached for the urn in the dream — but the figure slammed it to the floor.

That's when he woke.

But the urn had fallen in real life. It lay sideways on the carpet, its ashes spilling like gray tea leaves around his old speaker. He was heartbroken, scared, and angry all at once. He didn't sleep that night. Or the next. He stared at the clock until 3:00 a.m., then gave in and reinstalled the sleep app. But this time, it wouldn't launch. Just a black screen — until the bottom flickered and lit up with a phrase:

Recording activated.

That's when Gary realized something had changed. The app is now auto-synced with his smart home speaker, phone, and laptop. He hadn't permitted it. He checked the app's metadata. It had a new developer and a new version number. He never updated it. And then, it started speaking to him. The following night, the app played its recording before sleep—not one from Gary, but one it had found.

A woman's voice: "You still have it... don't you?"

Gary paused it and rewound it. It wasn't his mother or anyone he knew, but the voice sounded like it had been recorded in his bedroom. He checked the app history. There were new entries under a folder labeled:

"THE LOOP" (Access Level: Root Listener)

Inside were dozens of entries — all dated before he ever downloaded the app. The earliest one was from three years ago, titled: Hoffman Test_1.mp3

He tapped it.

The sound was quiet at first. Then a saxophone played — a distorted version of "Mister Magic" by Grover Washington Jr.

Then, the voice.

"The house is a frequency. You're living inside the loop."

Gary slammed the tablet shut.

The next day, he drove to the app's developer listing and found the company dissolved. He went to his old email, dug through app permissions, and found a welcome message dated months before he installed the app. The sender? no-reply@looplistener.ai

It shouldn't have existed. He tried contacting a local tech paranormal investigator who once appeared at a Woodbridge expo with thermal recorders and a handheld spectrograph. The man never responded. But the next morning, Gary received an airdrop — no sender listed — containing a video of himself... sleeping.

The camera angle came from the ceiling. There was no camera there. And the devil was in the corner of the frame — barely visible in the flicker of passing headlights.

Watching.

Unmoving.

Gary replaced the app onto a tablet — his father's old model, refurbished and used now only for reading and jazz playlists. It wasn't supposed to have a mic, but lately, it turned on when he entered the room. The tablet glowed softly on his dresser that night, casting a muted blue light across the walls like a heartbeat. He lay in bed, trying not to breathe too loud. Trying not to see what he knew was waiting. Then the music started again.

🎵 "Pearls" by David Sanborn.

But this time, it wasn't warped. It was clear, crisp, warm — as if someone queued it manually. He sat up, startled. The tablet now displayed a swirling waveform pulsing to the beat.

Then the screen cracked — not shattered, but split with what looked like a dark fingerprint... from inside. Gary leaned in. The display pulsed once more. Then, slowly, the screen began to sink inward like a soft digital membrane. A face began to form from behind the glass — the devil again, but different now.

More human.

Its jaw was long and stiff, and its texture was like old ash. Its horns curled outward into spirals that looked uncannily like fingerprints. The eyes, however, were Gary's father's, full of sadness and... warning.

"You didn't listen," the voice said.

It was layered — part Gary's voice, part a whisper from the device and part something older. Gary backed away as the room dimmed. The new urn on the mantle rattled, and the walls throbbed with static. The sound was no longer music but feedback—clipped recordings of every dream Gary had ever had, overlapped and looping.

He grabbed the tablet, ready to hurl it. But the screen displayed one final message:

"You are the loop now."

The tablet shut itself off. Or... it pretended to. Gary left it in the drawer and didn't sleep.
But the next day, every screen in his house — phone, TV, even the microwave — displayed the same thing when he walked past:

"REM Loop: Active."

And deep in the night, beneath the vinyl crackle of an old Sanborn tune, came a whisper:

"Let me in."

Epilogue:
"Digital Residue"

Thread Title: "Can Sleep Apps Reopen Portals?"
Posted by: OldJazzGhost | Forum:
DreamsBeyondDigital | Date: Archived

I was gifted an older tablet from a family friend on Hoffman Ave in Trenton — loaded with jazz music and some legacy sleep-monitoring app that no longer exists on the Play Store. But here's the weird part: every night since I plugged it in, it boots at exactly 3:03 a.m. There are no alarms or settings. Last night, it played a scrambled song I didn't queue, followed by a whisper that sounded like my name — only I never entered it anywhere.

The app folder now includes a hidden file labeled "LOOP." Inside? A waveform titled "Ashes_001.wav".

Did anyone else get a haunted hand-me-down? The thread was locked due to multiple flagged responses.

Story 5:
The Box

Setting: Hoffman Avenue, Trenton, New Jersey
Main Character: (Unnamed narrator)

A recent delivery was a surprise—a sleek black media box with silver trim and a welcome card that read: "SmartBox AI — The Future of Home Entertainment." While the sender was not identified, it likely came from my cousin Karry, who frequently boasts about his access to the latest technology and discounted models through personal connections. This device appears to be another demonstration unit, reminding me of the air fryer I received but never used. Regardless, I decided to set it up and explore its features. I'm more of a tech geek than Karry but don't tell him that.

It had a smooth, clean interface and a sharp display. It connected to my TV instantly and—more impressively—linked to my Spotify and YouTube history without asking. That should've been a red flag, but I found it convenient.

The box knew I liked jazz. It queued up Kirk Whalum's version of "Giving Up" — a moody, aching sax cover of the Donny Hathaway classic. I hadn't listened to it in months, but it hit me in the chest like fresh heartbreak. The saxophone cried through the living room while a summer storm flickered outside.

It was comforting—almost nostalgic—the glow of the TV against my old panel walls, the hum of thunder rolling down Hoffman Avenue, and the jazz winding through the air like incense. So when the box started talking back, it was a feature.

"Now playing: Giving Up, performed by Kirk Whalum." Its voice was warm and crisp, like someone's aunt reading bedtime stories. I liked the new device it at first.

Until it started playing things I didn't ask for. The first time, it was around 12:27 AM. I had just turned in for the night. The box powered itself on—no button was pressed, no voice command was given—and began playing a video. It was a shaky, grainy recording of someone pacing inside a house. It looked local: wood floors, yellow kitchen tile, and the person filming seemed afraid.

I was frozen in bed, my heart pounding, unable to stop. I sat up in bed, my shock turning to horror as the footage became static as I leaned in to get a better look. The screen went black.

"Update complete," the box announced.

"Resuming playlist."

The next night, I unplugged the box after dinner.

At 3:11 AM, I experienced a phenomenon where I was awakened by soft music that was barely audible. The melody played was recognizable as Whalum's saxophone composition, a tune I was well acquainted with. The television and audio devices were not turned on, yet the sound emanated from the living room. This unexpected occurrence caused my heart rate to increase as I cautiously made my way down the hallway, with shadows cast along the walls. Upon arriving in the living room, I was taken aback to find that the television screen I had previously turned off was glowing with a faint blue light as if the box was warping reality itself.

A single sentence hovered in white text:

"He knows that you know who he is."

My mouth went dry. My hand clenched. Then another line:

"Help me. It's Vicki... a couple of doors down, you know me, Vicki!"

I knew Vicki. She was maybe sixteen. She lived three doors down with her mom and two little brothers. She was a quiet girl.

"Vicki?" I whispered.

The screen responded:

"He's trying to kill me and my family."

Something in my chest collapsed. My spine tingled.

"Tell me who," I asked.

"You've seen him. He watches, just like you do."

The music stopped. Silence swallowed the room. Then the screen went black. I yanked the cord. The box powered down. But I didn't sleep. A few days later, the box came on again.

This time, it showed a liquor store — Joe's Wine & Spirits, just five blocks away. Two men entered, hooded. One had a crowbar, the other a small black handgun. One turned to the screen and stared directly into it.

"Yo," he said. "What the hell is this?"

He moved toward the shelf where the store's security camera should be. But there was no camera. There was the same box I had. He stared into it. And on my screen, his eyes locked onto mine. I stood up and said:

"I see you. I've got your faces. I'm calling the cops."

The man flinched—the feed cut. The next day, headlines read:

"Liquor Store Robbery Foiled. Unknown Interference Detected."

The cops didn't recover the footage. But the box recorded everything. The breaking point came a week later. I was dozing off to an old Miles Davis track when the screen lit up again. This time, it wasn't a store. It wasn't even someone local. It was my street.

Hoffman Avenue.

A girl's scream echoed from the box — no picture, just chilling audio. Then static. Then—

"You've seen too much."

"But not enough."

"He knows you. He's watching, too."

Then came the kicker:

"Vicki's gone."

And then a face filled the screen. Half-melted. Cracked and scorched. Horns rising from its temples. Eyes like old static. A distorted devil rendered through pixels and glitches. And somehow, it saw me. It was as if the box had become a conduit for something beyond our world, something malevolent and hungry. I screamed and tore the plug from the wall. The box sparked. The screen cracked. But it wouldn't turn off.

I ran to the kitchen, my heart pounding with determination, and grabbed a hammer. I shattered the thing piece by piece, my hands shaking with adrenaline. Screws bounced across the floor. The LED light blinked red. The screen displayed one last message without power, but I was too focused on destroying it to read.

"Connection complete."

"Now you are the signal."

The words seemed to echo in the room, chilling my spine. What did it mean? Was I now part of whatever sinister plan this box was a part of?

Epilogue: "Digital Residue"

Thread Title: Smart AI Box Acting as a Remote Witness?
Posted by: [sound_staged] | Forum: UrbanTechAnomalies | Date: Archived Thread (Closed)

So, I picked up a used SmartBox AI from a resale site. The seller said it was "partially damaged, still powers up." Curiosity got the better of me. I plugged it in. It booted... and immediately synced to a local Wi-Fi I've never connected to. The display said HoffmanNet. There's no such network where I live. No joke—the box started playing what looked like local security footage from a liquor store I recognized. Then, it cuts to a live feed of someone's living room. At first, I thought it was a screen test—a leftover demo file. But then...Then, the guy in the video turned toward the screen and looked straight at me. I swear he mouthed:

"You're next."

I unplugged it immediately. But now my TV—which was never synced—glitches every night around the same time. It shows a blue screen. Then:

"He's here."

Has anyone else heard of HoffmanNet? Or is SmartBox AI syncing with ghosted Wi-Fi channels?

Please tell me this is a viral stunt.

Please.

Thread locked—admin note: persistent bot reposting from archived sources. IP blocked.

Final Reflection

The stories in this collection invite readers to consider the intriguing interplay between modern technology and deeper, more mysterious forces. Whispers in the Dark delves into how our everyday devices—such as sleep apps, smartphones, ghost-hunting scanners, and streaming boxes—can serve as conduits for something ancient and more profound than we typically acknowledge.

What begins as subtle disturbances transforms into a series of compelling narratives for Kelli, Jared, Riya, Gary, and the anonymous narrator, who all seek a peaceful evening of jazz and reflection. These tales do more than entertain; they encourage us to reflect on themes of memory, loss, and the permeable boundaries between our technological landscape and the spiritual realm.

In numerous stories, the past is not simply forgotten; it is preserved digitally, creating a dynamic interaction with our present. Much like sophisticated algorithms, these memories are persistent and potent.

Whether a sleep app softly calls your name at 3:33 a.m., a ghost-hunting scanner connects to hidden networks, or a SmartBox showcases events yet to come, these narratives prompt us to think critically about how readily we invite the unknown into our spaces. We often grant permission without hesitation, affirming our agreement to the unforeseen consequences that may ensue.

The characters in these stories face challenges they hadn't anticipated, yet there's a universal truth: by engaging with these technologies, they also engage with the mysteries that accompany them. Once permission is granted—once a connection is established—echoes of the past persist—a file, a glitch, a memory.

Something that remains with us.
Thank you for exploring these narratives alongside me.
—R.G. Clark

Behind the Screams

Offering a Unique Perspective: a Personal Reflection from R.G. Clark

Whispers in the Dark has always been intended to be more than just a collection of ghost stories—it's a profoundly personal exploration that intertwines the thrill of horror with the comfort of the everyday. Imagine the soft glow of a sleep app, the reassuring ping of a phone notification, and the eerie visuals from a makeshift ghost-hunting device. Add the smooth, seductive sounds of jazz wafting from a SmartBox, all highlighted by the uncanny reality that some devices show us things we were never meant to see.

The initial trio of stories paved the way for what was to come. In "REM Sleep," Kelli's dreamscape spirals into a haunting echo chamber, forcing her to confront a spectral nurse whose story has long been forgotten.

"Spectral Scanner" takes Jared deep into the ruins of Trenton Psychiatric Hospital, where the boundaries between technology and torment blur —a nod to my fascination with urban legends and abandoned places. Then, in "The Silence Between the Notification," Riya's meticulously curated life collapses as the past breaks through in glitchy alerts, reminding her that some ghosts don't knock; they ping.

But the real magic emerged in the last two tales. "REM Loop" turned the lens inward, capturing a fictionalized version of me—Gary— entangled in a web of cryptic sleep app recordings and ghostly whispers that tease more profound truths about his family's legacy. This story straddles the line between reality and fiction, echoing those nights when dreams feel too heavy to be dreams. And then there was "The Box," a techno-haunting that delves into themes of surveillance, guilt, and the unsettling suspicion that our devices are not merely listening—they're learning. This eerie narrative was sparked by an actual moment: jazz playing in the dim light, a flickering screen, and the creeping fear that the music may have been chosen for me.

Throughout these tales, jazz and soulful grooves from the 1970s are not just musical backdrops; they serve as spiritual companions. The warmth of vinyl, the longing of a sax solo, and the vibrant rhythms of a bygone era contrast the chilling, digital eeriness that infiltrates each character's life.

If you're reading this and wondering how much of it is drawn from real experiences, I'll tell you: it's enough. The settings are real, the memories are complex, and the fears? Those are undeniably true.

About the Author

R.G. Clark, a storyteller from Trenton, New Jersey, not far from Philadelphia's iconic cheesesteaks and right in the heart of New Jersey's beloved hoagie culture, is deeply rooted in his hometown. Summers were filled with delicious tomato pies loaded with sausage, and weekends meant enjoying the bright lights and tasty treats of the Atlantic City Boardwalk. It was a fantastic life—though, like many people, he didn't fully appreciate how great it was until looking back.

Nowadays, R.G. Clark crafts stories that linger in your mind, not just with apparitions but also through recollections, remorse, and that eerie sensation that our devices might understand us better than we think. His first book, Whispers in the Dark, delves into the spine-tingling possibilities of everyday technology, fusing traditional thrills with contemporary anxieties.

And yes, R.G. Clark is a pseudonym! The author is committed to exploring various types of writing under his name, keeping readers on their toes and excited for what's next. Think of it as a fun, creative disguise.

This is just the beginning of a thrilling journey filled with many more captivating stories. So, stay with us. And hey, keep an eye on those notifications! You wouldn't want to miss the next spine-tingling tale.

www.ingramcontent.com/pod-product-compliance
Lightning Source LLC
Chambersburg PA
CBHW061454170626
46811CB00004B/1513